MY BOOK

Shags
Finds a Kitten

GYO FUJIKAWA

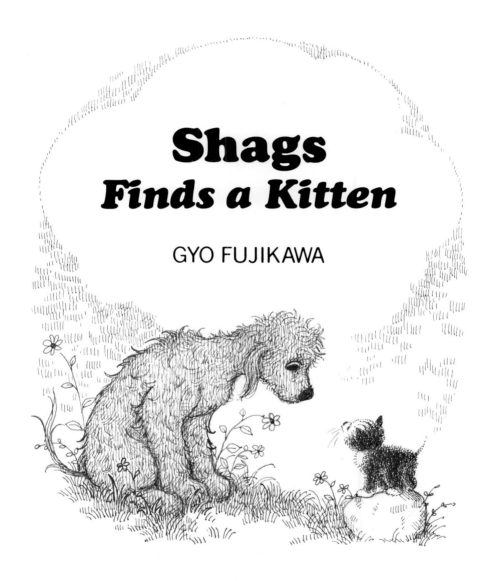

G R O S S E T   &   D U N L A P   ·   P U B L I S H E R S   ·   N E W   Y O R K

Library of Congress Catalog Card Number: 82-083739. ISBN: 0-448-16465-5.

Drip, drop, drip went the rain. Sam was curled up for the night, and his dog, Shags, was curled up under Sam's bed.

Sam yawned. "Good night, Shags."

Shags thumped his tail, and the rain went drip, drop, drip.

Drip, drop, "Meow!" Sam was sound asleep.

Drip, drop, "Meow!" Shags was wide awake.

Shags sniffed at the window. Something was out there!

Shags whined. Sam snored.
Then Shags pulled Sam's cover off
and licked his toes.
"Stop tickling me!" said Sam, rolling out of bed.

Shags ran back to the window again.
Sam came over and looked out. "See? There's nothing out there."
Drip, drop, "Meow!"
"Shags!" said Sam. "There's a kitten out there!"

But not for long. Sam and Shags brought her
into the kitchen.

Sam warmed up some milk, and the kitten stopped
meowing and began to purr while she lapped it up.

Then Sam fixed her
a soft bed in a shoe box
and got back into his bed.

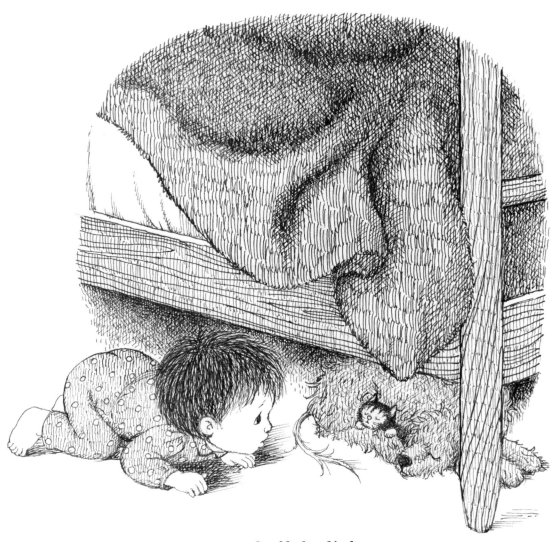

Before he turned off the light,
Sam looked over at the kitten. She was gone!
He looked under his bed. There she was
curled up with Shags.

In the morning Sam's friends Jenny,
Mei Su, and Nicholas came over to play.

They made a big fuss over the kitten.

"But you'll have to give her back," said Nicholas.

"Why would anyone put a kitten out in the rain?"
asked Sam.

"Maybe she ran away," said Jenny, "and somebody
is looking for her."

"Come on, Jenny," said Nicholas. "Let's walk around
and see if anybody lost a kitten."

"But they can't have her back unless they promise
to take real good care of her," said Mei Su.

Sam and Mei Su stayed behind with the kitten.
When Mei Su dressed her in a doll's bonnet,
she purred.

When Sam gave her a ride in his wagon,
she purred.

"If you keep her, what will you call her?"
asked Mei Su.

"Raindrop," said Sam, "because she dropped
out of the rain."

All this time Shags
was feeling left out.
Nobody put a bonnet
on him. Nobody pulled him
around in a wagon.

Shags brought his ball to Sam.
Sam wouldn't throw it.

Then he brought his ball to Mei Su.
But she didn't want to throw it, either.

In a little while Jenny and Nicholas
came back. Nobody they asked had lost a kitten.

Shags was lying under the lilac bush,
feeling very sorry for himself.

Raindrop trotted over to him—
she wanted to play! But when she pounced
on his tail, Shags yapped at her.

"Bad Shags!" yelled Sam.
Mei Su picked up the kitten and
put her in Sam's wagon.

Nicholas gave her Shags' ball to play with.
Nobody paid any attention to Shags.

Shags watched Raindrop chase the ball around
the wagon. All of a sudden the ball bounced out
and rolled under the lilac bush.

Raindrop scrambled down to get it back,
and the strings on her bonnet caught on a twig.
She squeaked as they tightened around her neck.

Shags barked for help.

"Quiet, Shags!" called Sam.

"Is he barking at Raindrop again?"
said Mei Su.

They all ran over to see.

There was Shags holding Raindrop very gently
in his mouth to keep her from choking!

"Poor little Raindrop," said Mei Su,
untangling the bonnet strings.
"Shags, you're a real hero!" said Sam.
"Good dog," said Jenny, and she
patted his head.

"Here, boy," said Nicholas, and he
gave Shags the ball.
Mei Su gave Shags a hug.
Shags was feeling a lot better.

"Hi! I heard you found my kitten."
A little boy carrying a basket was standing nearby.
Jenny spoke right up. "Why did you put a little
kitten out in the rain?"

"I didn't," said the boy. "She got lost."
"And you didn't miss her all night?" asked Nicholas.
"It isn't easy watching eight kittens,"
said the boy.

"Do you want her back?" asked Sam.

"Not if you promise to take good care of her," said the boy. "Will you help me find homes for her seven brothers and sisters?"

And that's exactly what they did.